Dear Parents and Educators,

Welcome to Penguin Young Readers! As parents and educators, you know that each child develops at his or her own pace—in terms of speech, critical thinking, and, of course, reading. Penguin Young Readers recognizes this fact. As a result, each Penguin Young Readers book is assigned a traditional easy-to-read level (1–4) as well as a Guided Reading Level (A–P). Both of these systems will help you choose the right book for your child. Please refer to the back of each book for specific leveling information. Penguin Young Readers features esteemed authors and illustrators, stories about favorite characters, fascinating nonfiction, and more!

Llama Llama™: Llama Llama Loses a Tooth

LEVEL 2

GUIDED READING LEVEL **I**

This book is perfect for a **Progressing Reader** who:
- can figure out unknown words by using picture and context clues;
- can recognize beginning, middle, and ending sounds;
- can make and confirm predictions about what will happen in the text; and
- can distinguish between fiction and nonfiction.

Here are some **activities** you can do during and after reading this book:
- Make Connections: Have you ever lost something? What did you do to try to find it?
- Sight Words: Sight words are frequently used words that readers must know just by looking at them. They are known instantly, on sight. Knowing these words helps children develop into efficient readers. As you read the story, have the child point out the sight words below.

her	his	over	put	then
him	of	pretty	some	when

Remember, sharing the love of reading with a child is the best gift you can give!

—Sarah Fabiny, Editorial Director
　Penguin Young Readers program

*Penguin Young Readers are leveled by independent reviewers applying the standards developed by Irene Fountas and Gay Su Pinnell in *Matching Books to Readers: Using Leveled Books in Guided Reading*, Heinemann, 1999.

PENGUIN YOUNG READERS

An Imprint of Penguin Random House LLC

Penguin supports copyright. Copyright fuels creativity, encourages diverse voices,
promotes free speech, and creates a vibrant culture. Thank you for buying an authorized edition
of this book and for complying with copyright laws by not reproducing, scanning, or distributing any
part of it in any form without permission. You are supporting writers and allowing Penguin
to continue to publish books for every reader.

Copyright © Anna E. Dewdney Literary Trust. Copyright © 2018 Genius Brands International, Inc.
Published by Penguin Young Readers, an imprint of Penguin Random House LLC,
345 Hudson Street, New York, New York 10014. Manufactured in China.

ISBN 9781524785024 (pbk)   10 9 8 7 6 5 4 3 2 1
ISBN 9781524785031 (hc)   10 9 8 7 6 5 4 3 2 1

PENGUIN YOUNG READERS

Level 2

PROGRESSING READER

llama llama™
loses a tooth

Anna Dewdney

based on the bestselling children's book series
by Anna Dewdney

Penguin Young Readers
An Imprint of Penguin Random House

Llama Llama carries a box
of his toys.

Mama Llama carries a box,
a bag, and a ball.
Crash!

"Sorry!" says Mama.

"I don't want to bump my

loose tooth," says Llama.

He wants it to fall out on its own.

He will put it under his pillow.

Llama smiles at Mama.

"Oh no, Llama. Your tooth already fell out!" Mama says. But where did it go?

They remember the places they
visited that day—

Nelly Gnu's house, Luna Giraffe's
house, Daddy Gnu's bakery, and
the park.

Mama hugs Llama. "Don't worry.

We'll look here first," she says.

Mama shakes Llama's

bed blanket.

Llama plays
while they look.
They have fun.
But they don't find
Llama's tooth.

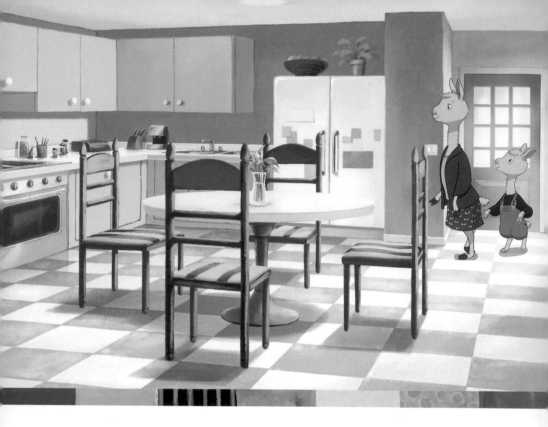

Next they look in the kitchen.

Llama sees his reflection

in the kettle.

His ears droop.

"Oh, where is my tooth?"

he moans.

Mama and Llama visit Nelly Gnu.

They look in her yard.

Llama finds an earthworm.

Llama finds a pretty pebble.

They swing high to look more.

Whee!

Whoopee!

They have fun.

But they don't find Llama's tooth.

Then they visit Luna.

"I found the tooth!" cries Nelly.

"Sorry," says Luna.

"Those are beads for my art."

Mama Llama hugs Llama.

"We'll keep looking," she says.

They visit Daddy Gnu's bakery.

The tooth is not there.

More friends join the hunt.

They go to the park.

They march around

and look for the tooth.

They have fun.

But they don't find

Llama's tooth.

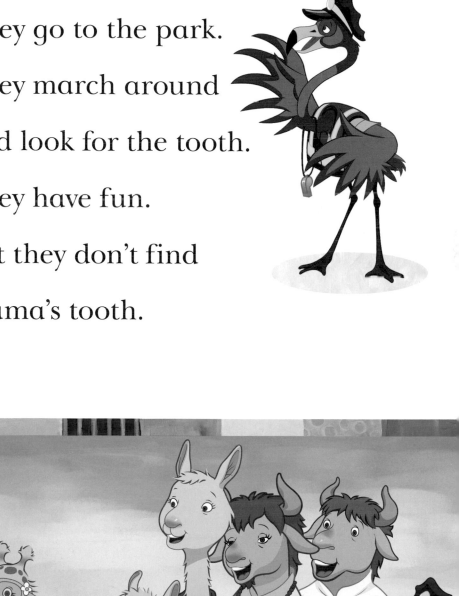

They look in the sandbox.

Harry the Arctic Hare helps, too.

"I found it!" calls Harry.

"But it is only a piece of shell."

Harry gives Llama ice cream to cheer him up.

Then Llama Llama remembers.

"We went to Gram and

Grandpa's house," he says.

There they check the yard
and kitchen.

They don't find Llama's tooth.

Everyone goes back to Llama's house to look some more.

They find many lost things.

But they don't find Llama's tooth.

Llama is sad at bedtime.

Then he hears music outside.

Gram is playing her flute.

Gram says, "My flute made awful
noises tonight.

And when I turned it over, look
what popped out!"

Gram hands it to Mama.

It's Llama Llama's tooth!

Then Llama remembers.

He blew on Gram's flute in her
kitchen!

His tooth must have fallen

out then.

Finally, Llama puts the tooth

under his pillow.

In the morning, Llama checks under his pillow.

The tooth is gone, but now there are coins instead.

"Yippee!" he cheers.